A Dragon Colorir For Girls

With Stories About Dragons, Unicorns, and Fairytale Creatures

Written by Ryan Robinson
Illustrations by Callie Robinson
Special Contributions by Cassidy Robinson

Willow and the Mysterious Tower

Willow was a baby dragon with a special love for the outdoors. She enjoyed the forests and meadows, walking through tall weeds, and discovering new and amazing things. One day, while out exploring, she stumbled across an old, neglected tower.

Willow was immediately drawn to the tower and decided to investigate. She crept closer and closer until she was right up against the wall. Her heart raced as she looked up to the top. She wanted to see inside the tower and find out what secrets it held.

She slowly climbed up, using her claws and wings to help her along the way. But the higher she got, the more difficult it became. The stones were old and crumbling, and the wind blew fiercely around her. Willow was determined to reach the top and see what was inside, so she kept going.

Finally, after what felt like hours of climbing, she reached the top. But the door was locked. Remembering she was a dragon, she used her fire breath to melt the lock and finally stepped inside. She could not believe her eyes!

What Happens Next?

_____

_____

_____

_____

_____

_____

_____

_____

Draw Your Story

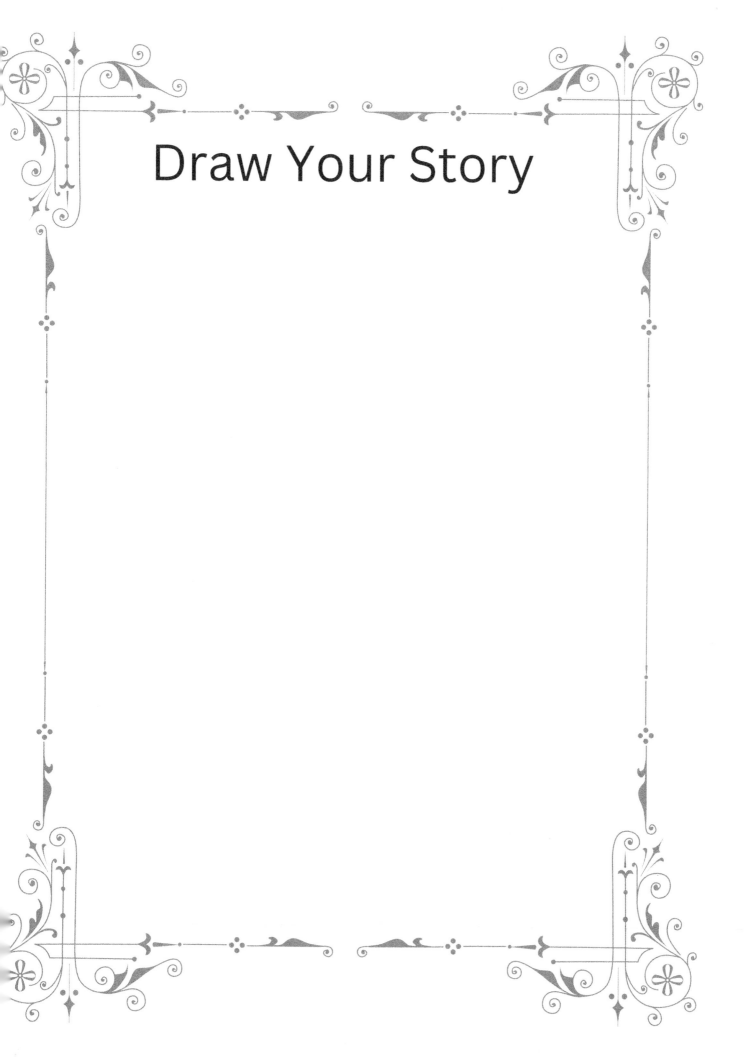

Rose's Friendship Quest

Rose was a teenage dragon who had been out on her own since she was a child. Growing up, she didn't have many friends and had been alone most of her life. One day, she decided it was finally time to leave home and go on a long journey.

As she walked, she saw the world in a different way. She loved the colors and smells of the meadows and forests. She watched intently as the animals went about their day. She noticed the differences in the terrain. She enjoyed climbing the hills and mountains and exploring the depths and hidden corners of the forests. She noticed the beauty of the wildflowers, the birds singing in the trees, and the sunlight filtering through the leaves. For the first time in her life she discovered something new and exciting around every corner.

As she walked along her way, she saw another dragon playing by herself. Not knowing if she would be friendly or not, Rose took a chance to introduce herself in a kind and gentle way. They talked for hours and Rose shared stories of her own life. The dragon opened up to Rose and told her about all of her worries and fears. Rose reassured her she was not alone and she could trust her.

After talking for several hours, Rose and her new friend decided to go on a new adventure together.

What Happens Next?

_____

_____

_____

_____

_____

_____

_____

Draw Your Story

A World Tour Adventure

Once upon a time, there lived a dragon and a unicorn in a magical land. The dragon's name was Drake and the unicorn's name was Jasmine. They were close friends who were always looking for new adventures together.

One day, Drake and Jasmine decided to take a trip around the world. The two friends set off with a bag full of supplies. The took along a map, a compass, a canteen of water, a few snacks, a first aid kit, some flashlights, a tent, a sleeping bag, a change of clothes, a fishing rod, and tools for repairing their equipment. They also grabbed a few coins to spend at the places they visited.

The first place they came to on their trip was a beautiful garden surrounded by tall trees. The garden was alive with the sound of birds chirping and the buzzing of bees. Wildflowers grew in abundance, and the sweet scent of cherry blooms filled the air.

They saw deer, rabbits, squirrels, and many other creatures. On the other side of the garden was a tremendous waterfall. They cautiously approached the waterfall and peered over the edge to see what was causing the noise. They could not believe what they saw!

What Happens Next?

_____

_____

_____

_____

_____

_____

_____

_____

Draw Your Story

The Griffin and the Unicorn

Once upon a time there lived together a griffin and unicorn in a magical kingdom. The griffin and unicorn spent their days exploring the kingdom, learning more about their magical powers, going on picnics together together, and finding ways to help their fellow creatures. They took long walks in the countryside and loved discovering new places and meeting new friends. They enjoyed playing games and sharing stories. Every day was a new adventure for the griffin and unicorn.

One day they heard rumors of a giant monster who was terrorizing the land. The monster had red eyes, sharp claws, and thick black fur. The monster's roar was loud and sounded like thunder. The monster was destroying villages and stealing everyone's food and gold. The monster was also using it's powerful magic to create storms making the land dangerous for everyone.

The griffin and unicorn knew they had to act fast. They could not allow this monster to destroy everything they loved. They decided to set off on a quest together in order to save the land and the kingdom from the terrible monster.

What Happens Next?

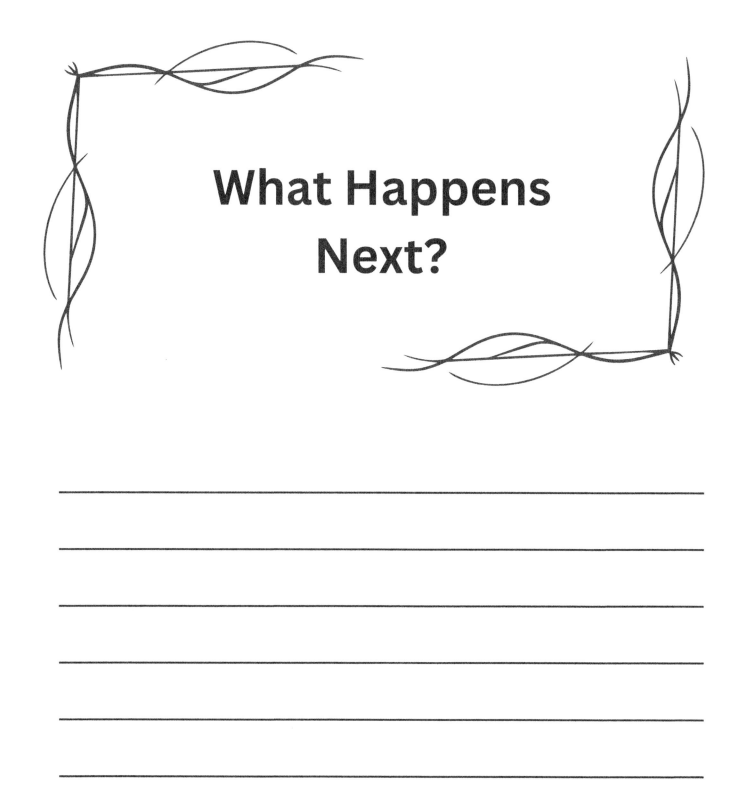

_____

_____

_____

_____

_____

_____

_____

Draw Your Story

The Pegasus and the Golden Key

Far away and long ago there lived a pegasus named Skye. Skye loved exploring, learning new secrets, and telling others about her new discoveries. One day, while playing with her friends by the creek, she spotted something sparkling in the water. Peering into the water, she discovered a sparkling golden key.

The key was studded with glittering rubies and sapphires and was intricately carved out of a bright golden material. The key was in the shape of a heart. Skye wondered what the key could possibly open.

Hoping someone else knew the answer, Skye went around town asking everyone she could. But no one had ever seen the key. Finally, she wondered if someone older may have seen the key long ago. She decided to ask her grandmother.

Immediately her grandmother recognized the key and told her the legend behind it. "Long ago, there was a pegasus with a very special secret. The pegasus did not want the secret falling into the wrong hands, so she asked a unicorn to seal it up with a magic door that only this key can open. No one knows where the entrance is, but whoever finds it will unlock an amazing secret.

The little pegasus was excited to find the hidden door. She searched far and wide, but had no luck. Finally, she returned to the creek where she found the key. She was about to throw the key back when she noticed a strange tree on the other side. As she flew over to it, the key began to glow. Bringing the key closer, it grew brighter and brighter until it vanished. The pegasus looked to the tree which had become a door opening into a room. And inside the room was the secret her grandmother had described!

What Happens Next?

_____

_____

_____

_____

_____

_____

_____

_____

Draw Your Story

Daisy and the Land Without Magic

Once upon a time, in a fairytale realm, there was a small fairy named Daisy. Daisy lived in a magical kingdom--a wondrous place filled with lush green forests, towering snow-capped mountains, and sparkling rivers winding their way through the landscape. The air was sweet with the scent of wildflowers, and the sky was filled with bright stars that glittered in the night. Everywhere, magical creatures roamed, from dragons perched atop the highest peaks to unicorns galloping through the meadows.

Daisy loved her home but she was curious about the outside world and longed to explore it. She wanted to discover new places and meet new creatures. But most of all, she was ready for a new adventure.

One day, Daisy decided to take a journey to a land without magic. She knew it would be a dangerous journey, but she was determined to explore the unknown. She spread her wings and flew off into the sky. As she flew, her wings created a soft breeze that blew through her long hair, and she twisted and turned as she glided through the air.

For days, Daisy flew through the sky, soaring over vast oceans and distant lands. Eventually, she came across a strange land--the land without magic. Without any magic, Daisy was feeling weak, but she pushed forward, determined to explore this strange new world. As she flew over the land, she noticed a small village tucked away in the corner. She slowly descended, and as she got closer, she could see the people of the village looking up at her with excitement. They had never seen a fairy before.

What Happens Next?

_____

_____

_____

_____

_____

_____

_____

_____

Draw Your Story

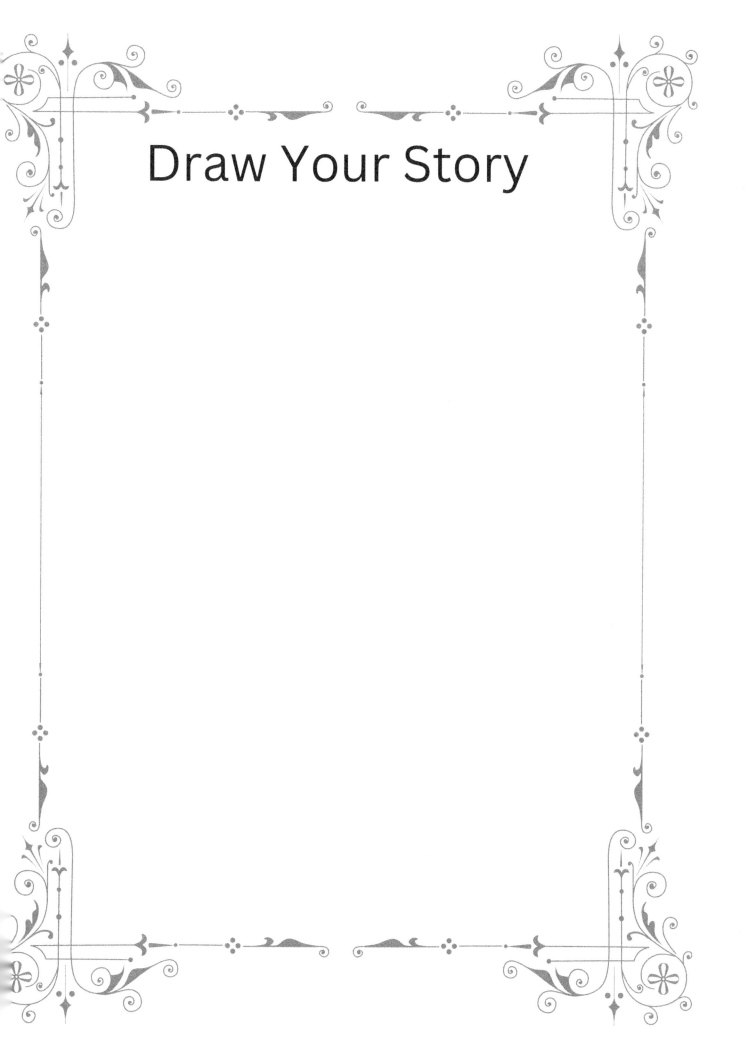

The Quest for the Underwater Kingdom

Once upon a time, there lived three friends in a magical kingdom. The three friends were a pixie named Blossom, a sprite named Fern, and a dryad named Tink. Although they grew up together, Blossom, the pixie, was the clear leader of this group.

Pixies by nature are a bit mischievous.So when Blossom heard about a mysterious underwater kingdom, she had no problem convincing her two friends to explore it. They planned their trip for weeks. Although Blossom and Fern could fly quite well, Tink could not. Plus, the journey across the sea would be way too far to fly. Unless they found an island somewhere there would be no place to stop and rest. So they knew they would need to set sail with their sailing boat.

For weeks they planned their trip. They gathered all the supplies they would need for their journey and set off on a bright and sunny day. The wind blew gently, and the sky was clear. The friends cheered with excitement as they hoisted the sails and glided through the calm waters of the harbor.The cool waves gently lapped at the sides of the boat. With the sun high in the sky, the sailboat cleared the harbor and in no time the friends found themselves out in the open sea. The wind now blew steadily with the giant sails propelling the boat forward. The friends watched in awe as the shoreline gradually disappeared behind them as they set off on their journey.

They took turns steering the ship and telling stories of their past adventures. They remembered the time they found the hidden treasure in a cave and how they solved the riddle in the enchanted forest. They recalled how they once outwitted a mean dragon and how they escaped from a maze of thorns. As the days went by, the friends grew closer together and more determined to find the underwater kingdom.Little did they know, a storm was brewing on the horizon and their adventure was about to take an unexpected turn.

What Happens Next?

_____

_____

_____

_____

_____

_____

_____

Draw Your Story

Lady Sabrina and the Fire Dragon

Once upon a time, there was a brave warrior named Lady Sabrina. Lady Sabrina enjoyed listening to the tales her father told her about his journeys and the adventures of travelers he knew. She learned about a powerful creature that guarded a magical jewel. The powerful creature's name was the Fire Dragon.

After hearing about this creature, Lady Sabrina was determined to find the dragon and prove her courage. She was warned the Fire Dragon was a dangerous creature

Lady Sabrina traveled for many days and came across a variety of strange creatures. One night, as she was camping in the forest, she heard a loud roar. She knew it was the Fire Dragon.

She ventured away from her camp and suddenly came face to face with the Fire Dragon. To her surprise, she immediately felt a connection with the beast. She then noticed it had a small jewel hanging around its neck. Lady Sabrina knew she had to get the jewel but she was scared to approach the dragon. She then remembered the tales her mother had told her about the Fire Dragon and how it only responds to courage. She took a deep breath and slowly stepped closer. The Fire Dragon felt her courage and instead of attacking, it bowed its head to her. Lady Sabrina carefully reached out and retrieved the jewel from around the dragon's neck.

What Happens Next?

_____

_____

_____

_____

_____

_____

_____

_____

_____

Draw Your Story

The Phoenix and the Pegasus

Once upon a time, there lived a phoenix named Saffron and her loyal pegasus friend Starfire. Saffron was a beautiful phoenix with bright red and orange feathers. She had piercing yellow eyes and a fiery spirit. She was brave, determined, and wise beyond her years. Starfire was strong with a sleek black coat, white mane and a long tail. She was brave and loyal, and always willing to lend a helping hoof to those in need. Starfire was a faithful companion to Saffron, and together they had a love for adventure.

One day, they set out on a journey to explore a mysterious island far away from their home. As they flew across the island, they encountered all sorts of magical creatures. They saw sprites dancing in a meadow below, a griffin soaring through the sky, and a unicorn running through a forest.

Soon, they came across a beautiful lake. The lake was a deep aquamarine color reflecting the night sky across its surface. The water was crystal clear and the moonlight cast a beautiful reflection on its surface. The lake was surrounded by lush green trees and bright flowers. Near the lake, they found a group of mermaids swimming and singing. Both Saffron and Starfire were mesmerized by their beauty.

They flew through the night, eventually coming to a majestic castle and a busy village. The castle was a towering structure made of grey stone and surrounded by a high wall. It was lit up by torches and had a large drawbridge leading to the entrance. Inside the castle, the walls were decorated with tapestries, and the floors were covered in plush carpets. Immediately, they both knew they had to explore the castle.

What Happens Next?

_____

_____

_____

_____

_____

_____

_____

_____

Draw Your Story

A Girl and Her Dragon

Once upon a time, in a village far away, there lived a brave little girl named Mia. She was known for her adventurous spirit and love for exploring the forest around her village.

One day, while playing in the woods, Mia stumbled upon a baby dragon. The dragon was crying and seemed lost. Mia felt sorry for the baby dragon and decided to take care of it. She fed it, played with it, and even gave it a name: Sparky.

However, soon the news of a dragon in the village spread, and people were afraid. They believed dragons were dangerous and could harm the village. So they asked Mia to get rid of the dragon.

Mia loved Sparky and didn't want to abandon him. So she came up with a plan to convince the villagers that not all dragons are dangerous.

She invited the villagers to a picnic in the forest and brought Sparky along. At first, the villagers were afraid, but Mia showed them Sparky was friendly and playful. She even taught Sparky some tricks, like blowing smoke rings and doing a little dance.

The villagers were amazed and soon realized dragons weren't as scary as they imagined. They apologized to Mia for their fear and accepted Sparky as a friend.

From that day on, Sparky became the village's mascot, and Mia and Sparky's bond grew stronger. They continued to explore the forest together, and Mia became known as the girl who tamed the dragon.

The end.

What Happens Next?

_____

_____

_____

_____

_____

_____

_____

Draw Your Story

Visit us on the web at:

www.ryansschool.com

Printed in Great Britain
by Amazon

43133767R00024